Lothrop, Lee & Shepard Books   New York

Library of Congress Cataloging in Publication   Smith, Maggie. Argo—You Lucky Dog / written and illustrated by Maggie Smith.   p.   cm.   Summary: When Argo the dog wins the lottery, he finds out what money is and starts making decisions about how to spend his new wealth.   ISBN 0-688-12052-0. —ISBN 0-688-12053-9 (lib. bdg.)   [1. Dogs—Fiction.   2. Wealth—Fiction.   3. Money—Fiction. 4. Lotteries—Fiction.]   I. Title.   PZ7.S65474Ar   1993   [E]—dc20   92-12891   CIP   AC

for Stephen

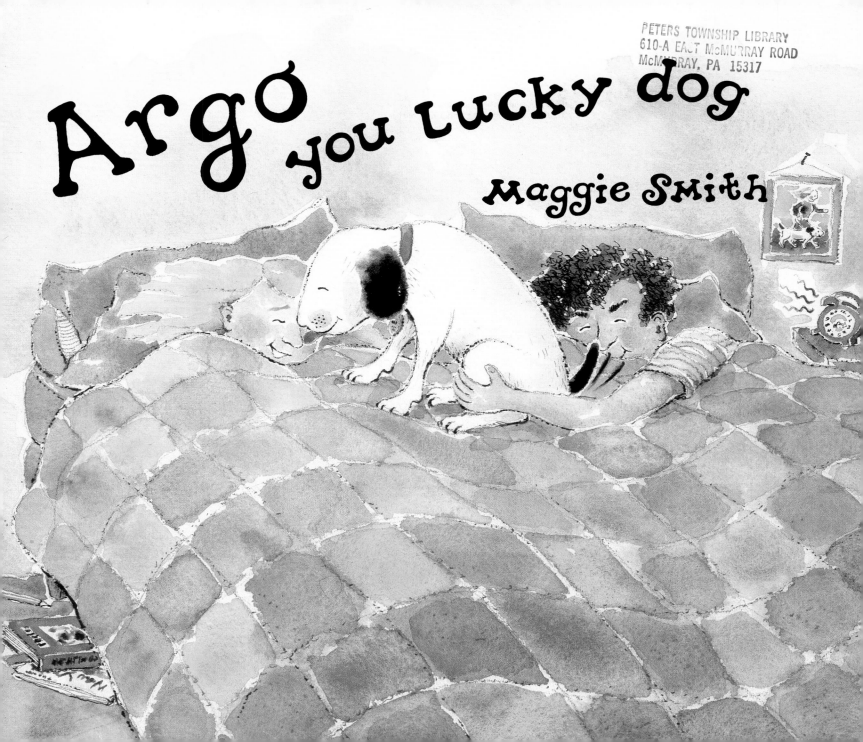

Argo
you lucky dog

Maggie Smith

IT WAS JUST ANOTHER MONDAY. Argo was making his downtown rounds to see what people might have dropped in the early morning bustle. "Nothing much," he thought, as he picked up a shiny red bottle cap, a sugar packet, and an old lottery ticket.

When he got home, Bob and Glynis were packing up the car.
"Sorry pal, it's a business trip," said Bob. "Can't take you with us this time."
"There's five days' worth of food," said Glynis. "Don't eat it all at once!
You be a good dog. We'll see you Friday night."

"What am I going to do by myself for five whole days?"
Argo wondered as he watched the car disappear.
He decided to read the paper. On page three he read this notice:

WINNING LOTTO TICKET STILL MISSING!
Officials seek the jackpot winner
Come on down to MIM'S —
news and candies and magazines
and of course, your LOTTERY CENTER

Argo remembered the ticket he'd found earlier.
He picked it up and trotted down to Mim's.

The woman behind the counter looked at the ticket and fed it through the lottery machine. She made a quiet phone call, then she turned back to Argo. "Well," she said. "This is a most unusual situation, but you certainly do have the winning ticket! The money will be delivered to your house this afternoon."

Argo went home to wait.

A few hours later, Argo's fortune arrived
in seventeen ten-pound sacks.

He stored them as quickly as possible,
but it took the rest of the day.

By evening he was hungrier than usual, so he ate one-and-a-half suppers.
Then he went to bed and dreamed of how he'd spend his fortune.

The next morning Argo was horrified to see the mess he'd made of the yard. "I'll have to do something about this," he thought. "It's a good thing I won the lottery."

It was a full day's work…

...but Argo was pleased with the results. "Glynis will love it!" he thought as he sniffed the red roses.

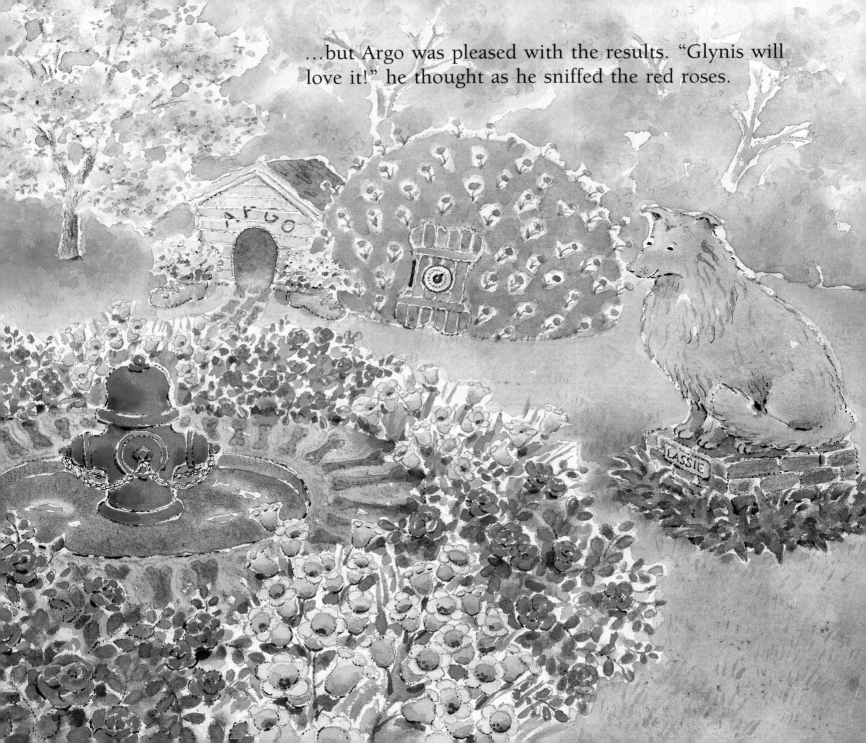

He ate another one-and-a-half suppers
and went to bed.

Wednesday was bright and sunny. As Argo admired the new yard, he couldn't help but notice how drab the house looked in comparison. "I'm going to fix that," he decided.

Felicia's
PAINTING
&
DECORATING
2__-2044

It took all day.

By dinnertime Argo was so hungry
he ate the two remaining suppers.
Then he went to bed.

When Argo got up on Thursday morning he didn't recognize himself. "Boy, do I need a bath!" he thought. He'd always found Bob and Glynis's bathtub a bit small for an enjoyable wash, but he had an idea.

"Bob will love it!" he thought as he took the first plunge.

After his long swim Argo was famished,
but his food bowls were all empty.
He decided to order out.

"Oh, my," thought Argo when the food arrived.
"It's more than I expected. I think I'll need some help."

He called over a few friends.

Friday morning Argo awoke with a start.
"Look at this mess," he thought. "I've got to get it
cleaned up before Bob and Glynis get home!"

"Easy come, easy go," Argo thought as he spent his last dollar.

The sun was just setting when Bob and Glynis came home.
"Hello, my sweet Argo," said Glynis. "We missed you so much!"
"I see you kept yourself busy while we were away," Bob added.

And they all went inside for their supper.